One night,
when everybody else was asleep...

Tom was still awake, reading with his torch.
He had nearly finished his book

when a huge hand tried to steal his Teddy!
But Tom wouldn't let go.

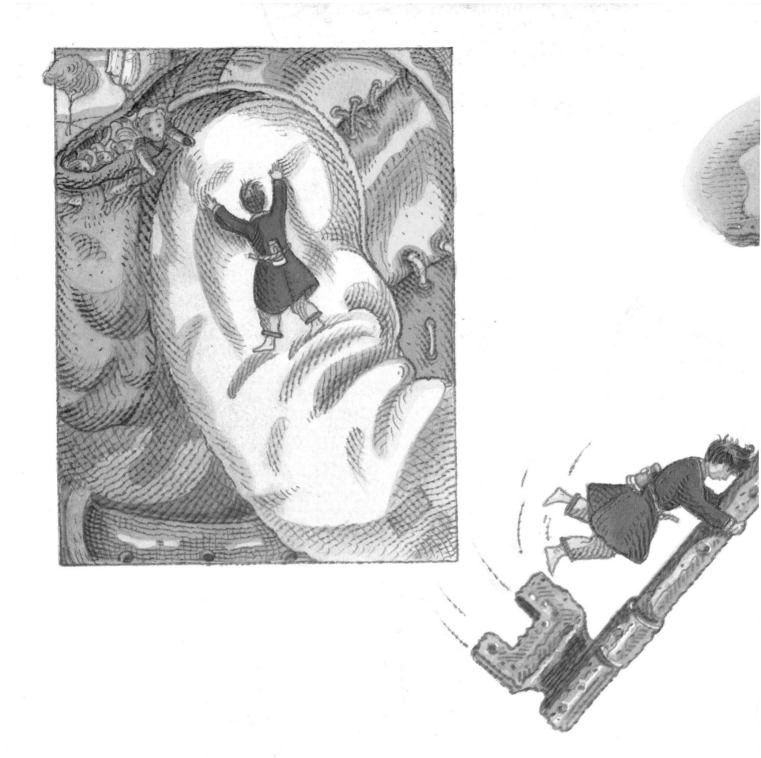

Tom's Teddy was pulled through
the window and thrown into a sack.
Tom tried to hold on, but he slipped
down a massive arm,
swung on a big iron key

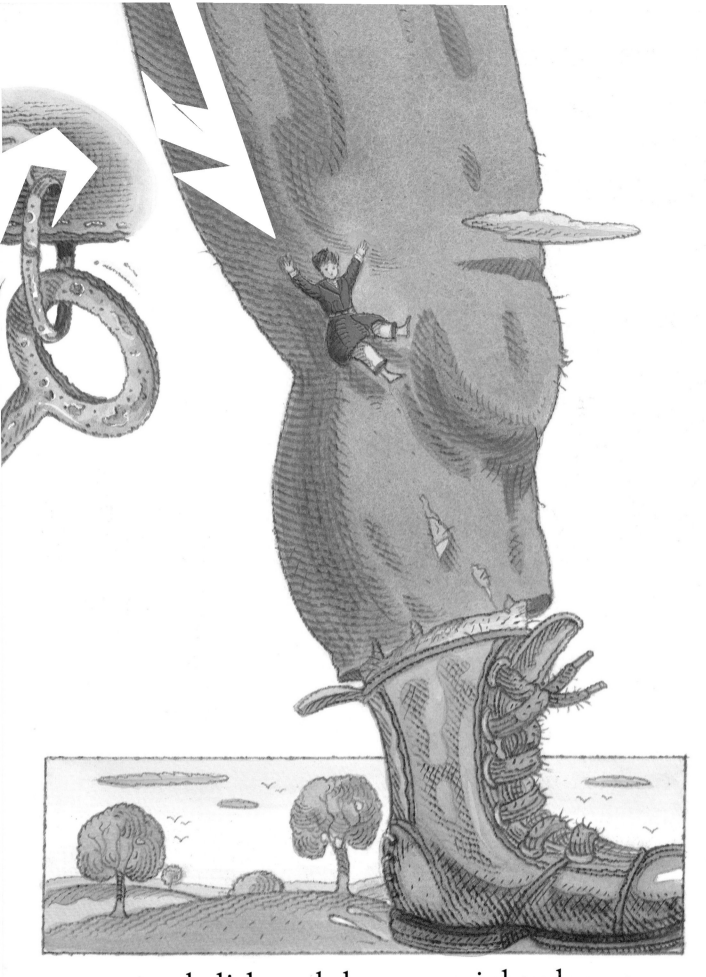

and slithered down a mighty leg.

The Teddy Robber was a GIANT!

Off went the Giant with great long strides,
while Tom clung on tight to a boot-strap.

They came to the Giant's castle.

Tom clambered up the steep steps
after the Giant...

...higher, and higher, and higher,
and higher...

until they came to a giant door.

Through the door was a vast room.

Tom climbed up the huge table leg, and
saw the giant with the sack of stolen Teddies.

The Giant picked up the Teddies one by one.

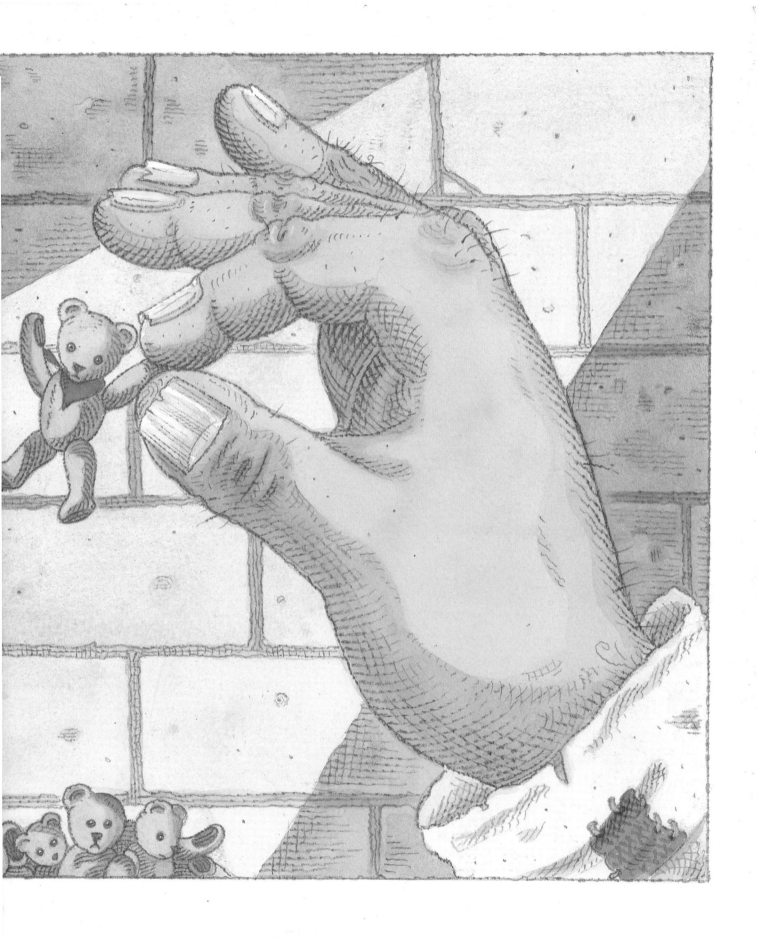

He looked at each bear *very* carefully.

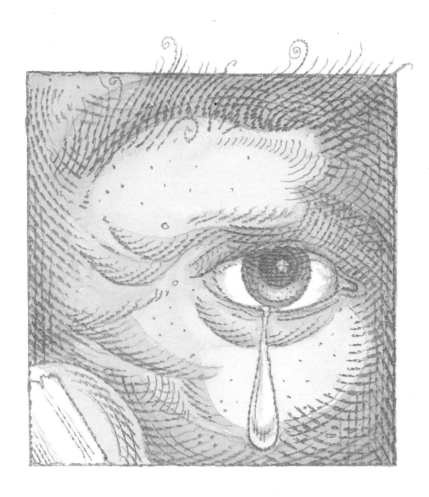

Then the Giant sighed a great sigh
and shed a single salty tear.

He picked up all the Teddies
and a big iron key.

He took the key to a huge padlock
on a huge cupboard.

Inside were…

all the lost Teddies in the world.

The Giant locked the cupboard.
Then he turned round and saw Tom.
'Who are you?' he boomed.
'I'm Tom and you stole my Teddy!'

'I've lost *my* Teddy,' wailed the Giant,
'that's why I'm the Teddy Robber.'
And he sat down on his bed and sobbed.
'Cheer up,' said Tom. 'Blow your nose,
and I'll help you look for him.'

They looked under the bed.

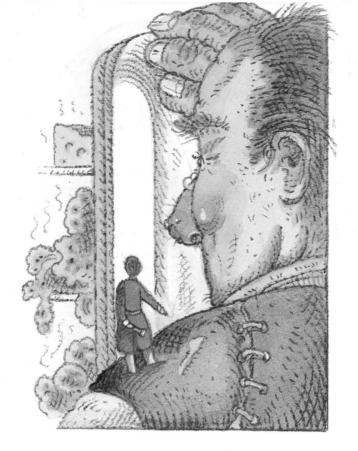

They looked in
the fridge.

They looked in
the cupboards.

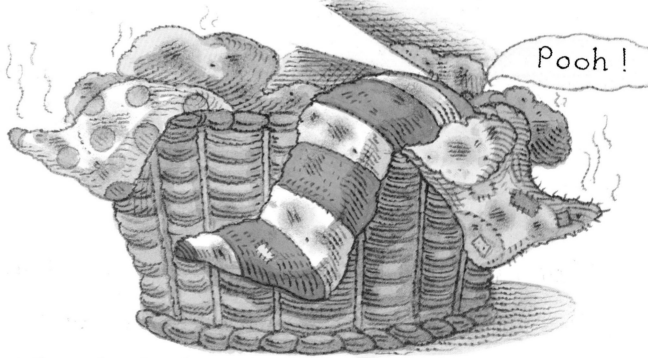

They looked in the dirty clothes basket.
They looked everywhere.

'We'll never find it,' said the Giant, and they sat down and had a mug of cocoa together. 'Would you like a biscuit?' asked the Giant politely.

'The biscuits are on your pillow,' said Tom. The Giant looked surprised. 'They ought to be on the shelf — the pillow is where my Teddy used to be.' And he began to cry all over again.

'If the biscuits are on your pillow,' said Tom,
'then perhaps your Teddy is...'

'...on the shelf!'

'My Teddy! My Teddy! You've found him!
How can I ever thank you?'
'First you can give me back *my* Teddy
and then you must put back all those stolen
Teddies — straight away!' said Tom.

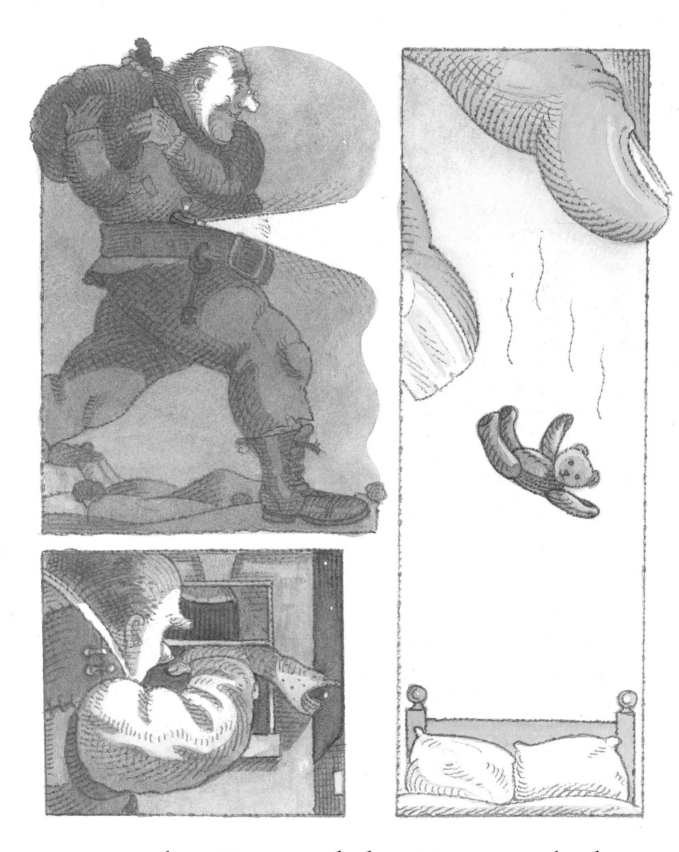

So together Tom and the Giant worked
all through the night to put the lost
Teddies back in their beds.

When they had finished, Tom went safely to bed
with his Teddy...

...and the Giant cuddled up with his Teddy
and was soon fast asleep.